CHICKEN SOUP FOR THE LITTLE SOULS

3 Colorful Stories to Warm the Hearts of Children

Story Adaptations by Lisa McCourt

Illustrated by Pat Grant Porter, Bert Dodson and Mary O'Keefe Young

Health Communications, Inc.
Deerfield Beach, Florida

www.hci-online.com
www.chickensoup.com

Library of Congress Cataloging-in-Publication Data

McCourt, Lisa.
[Chicken soup for the soul family storybook collection]
Chicken soup for the little souls: 3 colorful stories to warm the hearts of children / story adaptations by Lisa McCourt; illustrated by Pat Grant Porter, Bert Dodson, and Mary O'Keefe Young.
p. cm.
Contents: The goodness gorillas—The best night out with dad—The never-forgotten doll.
ISBN 1-55874-812-1 (trade paper)
1. Conduct of life—Juvenile fiction. 2 Children's stories, American. [1. Conduct of life—Fiction. 2. Short stories.] I. Porter, Pat Grant, ill. II. Dodson, Bert, ill. III. Young, Mary O'Keefe, ill. IV. Title.

PZ7.M13745 Ch 2000
[E]—dc21

00-035111

ISBN 1-55874-812-1

This collection was previously published in individual hardcover editions as:
Chicken Soup for Little Souls: The Goodness Gorillas, ©1997 Health Communications, Inc., ISBN 1-55874-505-X
Chicken Soup for Little Souls: The Best Night Out with Dad, ©1997 Health Communications, Inc., ISBN 1-55874-508-4
Chicken Soup for Little Souls: The Never-Forgotten Doll, ©1997 Health Communications, Inc., ISBN 1-55874-507-6

This collection was previously published together in a trade paperback edition as: *Chicken Soup for the Soul Family Storybook Collection,* ©1998 Health Communications, Inc., ISBN 1-55874-642-0

Produced by Boingo Books

Publisher: Health Communications, Inc.
3201 S.W. 15th Street
Deerfield Beach, Florida 33442-8190

The Goodness Gorillas:

For the real Jessica Docksteader and her mother, Christina, whose acts of love and kindness make the world a nicer place.
—Lisa McCourt

For my Jessica Porter Hays.
—Pat Grant Porter

The Best Night Out with Dad:

For Mike McCourt, a dad who knows how to make the best nights.
—Lisa McCourt

For Sydney, Riley and Emily.
—Bert Dodson

In memory of S. Wayne Clark. "Any male can be a father, but it takes a special man to be a dad."
I miss you, Dad.
—Dan Clark

The Never-Forgotten Doll:

For Bettye McCourt and Polly and Robert Hogan, with all the love in a once-little girl's heart.
—Lisa McCourt

For Ora and Dana, for allowing me to share their beauty with the world.
—Mary O'Keefe Young

The Goodness Gorillas

Story Adapted from
"Practice Random Acts of
Kindness
and Senseless Acts
of Beauty"
by Adair Lara

Story Adaptation by
Lisa McCourt

Illustrated by
Pat Grant Porter

It started the day Jessica Docket brought cupcakes to school for the whole class.

"Jessica!" said Ms. King. "I didn't know it was your birthday."

"It's not. My mom made cupcakes because she's a gorilla."

Jessica handed Ms. King a note.

Dear Ms. King
Thank you for letting me practice guerrilla goodness on your class.
Ms. Docket

Ms. King wrote these words on the chalkboard: guerrilla goodness.

guerrilla
goodness
butterflies

She told the class, "We all know what a gorilla is. But this word, guerrilla, means something else. It's a word that people use when they are part of a group that is trying to change something."

"Like a secret club?" asked Patricia.

"Sort of like that. Guerrilla goodness means practicing random acts of kindness. That's what Ms. Docket and lots of other people all over the world are doing right now. They're trying to make the world a nicer place just by finding new ways to be extra kind and good to people—even to strangers."

"You mean Ms. Docket makes cupcakes for strangers, too?" asked Stuart.

"She might. Or she might let someone in front of her in line at the grocery store . . .

NEW

"She might shovel snow from her neighbors' driveways without saying anything. She might plant flowers in a public place for everyone to enjoy, or help poor people. There are lots of ways to spread goodness once you start looking for them."

At lunchtime, everyone was talking about guerrilla goodness.

"Real gorillas in the jungle do nice things for each other, too," said Tina. "I saw it on TV."

"Let's make our own club!" said Michael. "Jessica should be the leader since she knows the most about it."

And that's how the Goodness Gorillas started.

Peter came to school early and sharpened all his classmates' pencils. Everyone smiled and said, "Thanks, Peter!"

Everyone except Todd. He tried to poke Peter in the arm with his pencil's new sharp point.

Jessica pulled out a mat for every person in her gymnastics class. "What a lovely act of kindness," said her coach.

Stuart let his little sister watch her favorite TV show, even though it was his turn to choose the channel. Later that night, his sister gave him the last piece of her Halloween candy.

All of the Goodness Gorillas met on Sunday and cleaned up the litter in the park. They were having a great time until Todd showed up with his scary dog, Brutus.

Todd walked over to the pile of cans the Goodness Gorillas had gathered for recycling.

He picked them up, and threw them all over the park. "Hey, dumb Gorillas, go fetch!" he yelled.

The Goodness Gorillas picked up all the cans again, but it wasn't as much fun as it had been before.

Patricia cleaned her room and her brother's room without being asked. Her dad thanked her and made her favorite dinner.

Tina packed up all her old toys, and her mom helped her bring them to a homeless shelter. "I'm so proud of you," said her mom.

Michael went with his uncle to volunteer at a senior citizen's home. A lady there told him, "You made our day."

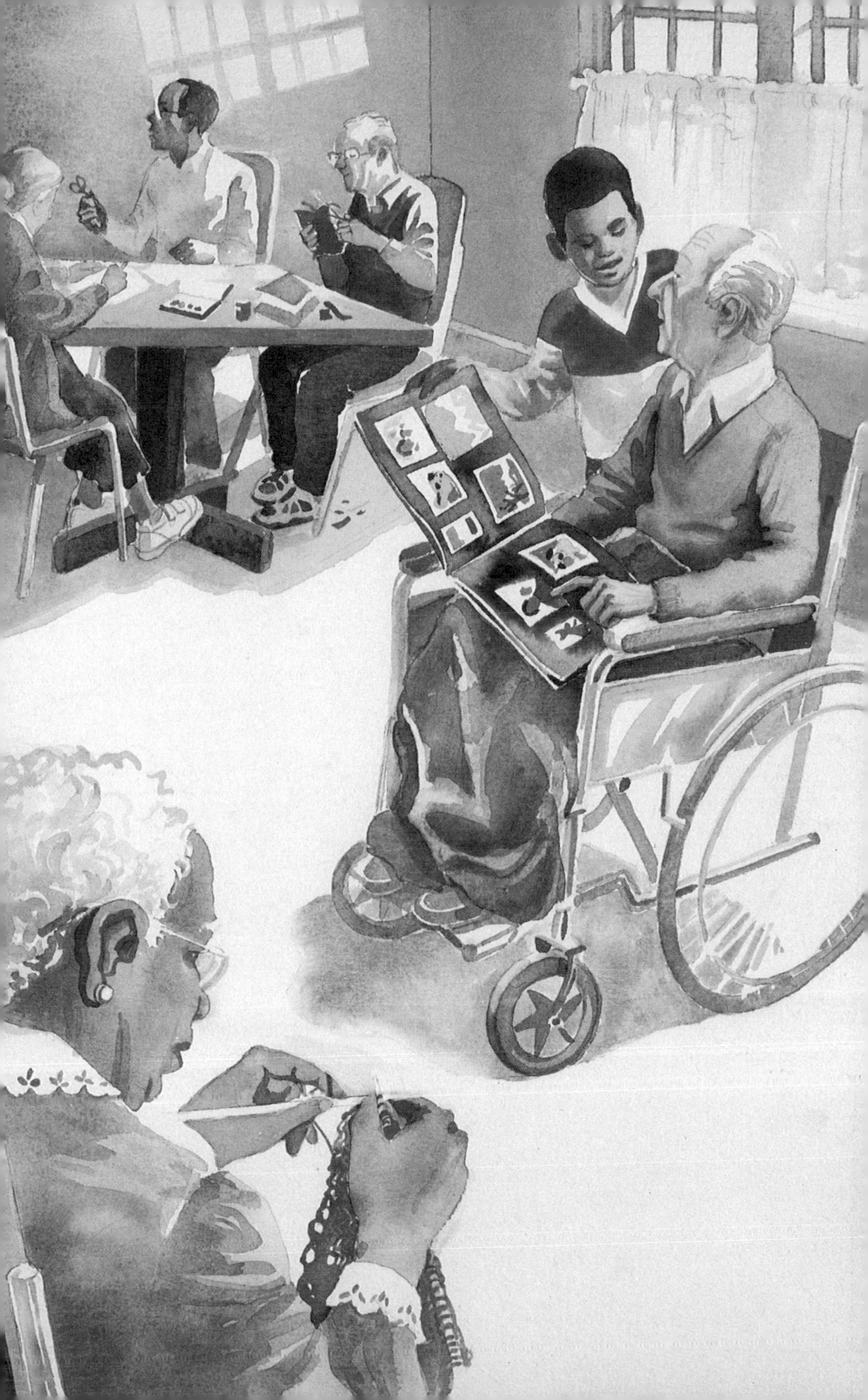

The Goodness Gorillas met at recess every day to talk about new ideas for spreading kindness. And every day Todd danced around the group, grunting and scratching his armpits.

"Oo—oo—oo—oo! Look at me—I'm a gorilla! I'm a big, dumb gorilla who makes goody-good with everyone!"

"What a creep," said Stuart. "All he ever does is cause trouble."

"Go away, Todd!" said Jessica. "If you can't be nice, we don't want you around."

One day, Ms. King said, "I have some sad news, class. Yesterday afternoon, Todd's dog, Brutus, was hit by a car. He died in the night. Todd is at home feeling bad and very alone. I'm hoping some of you will visit him. Does that sound like a job for the Goodness Gorillas?"

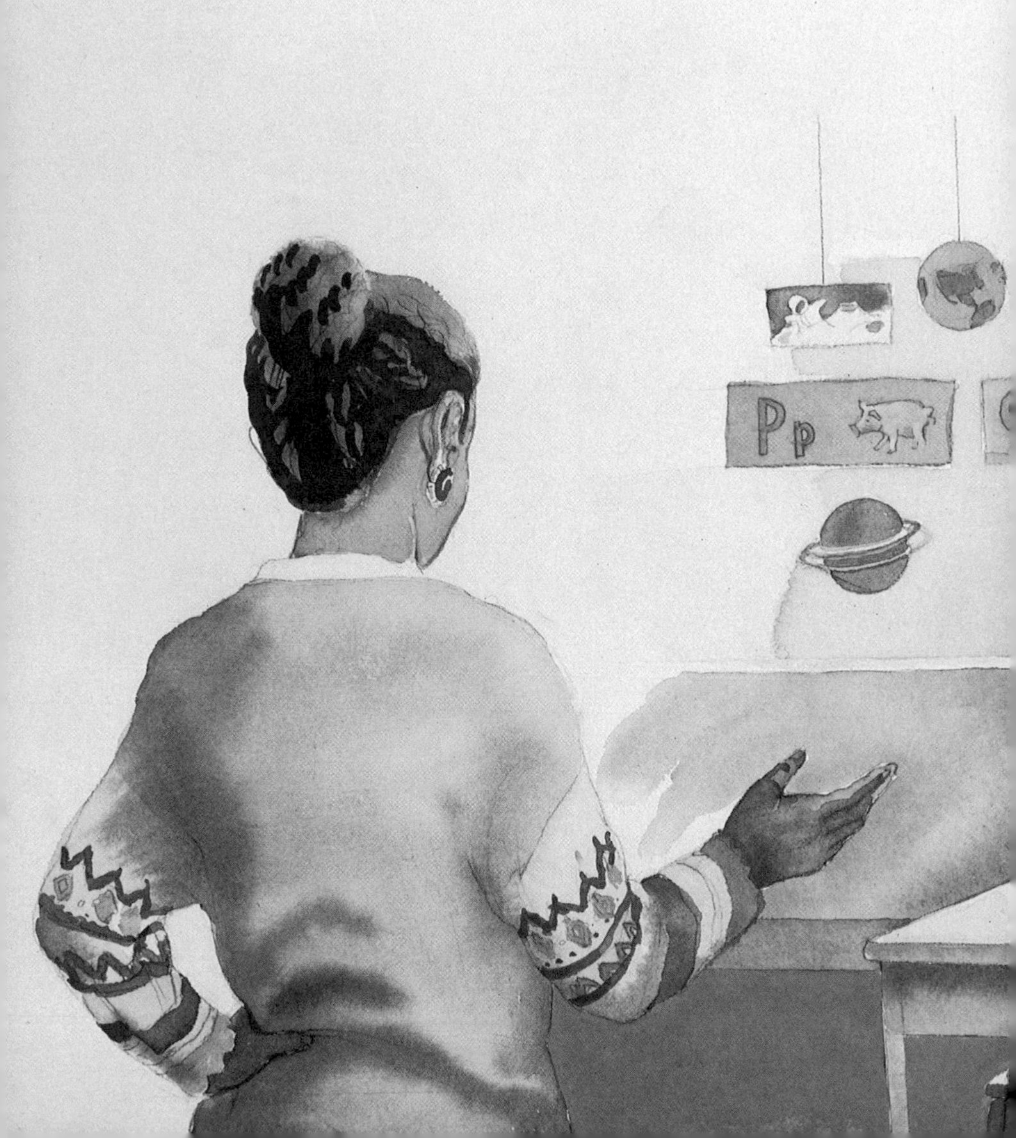

Jessica raised her hand. "It's just that . . . Todd makes fun of us so much. I wouldn't know what to say if we visited him."

"Maybe he's felt left out," said Ms. King. "Did any of you ever ask Todd if he'd like to join your club?"

"He's not a Goodness Gorilla!" cried Tina. "He's a Meanness Monster!"

"Goodness Gorillas see the good in everyone," said Ms. King. "Isn't that what you told me, Jessica?"

At recess, the Goodness Gorillas tried to decide what to do. Even though he'd been rotten, they all felt really bad for Todd. Brutus was his only friend.

"I know!" said Jessica. "My mom could take us to the pound to find a new dog for Todd!"

"Except," said Peter, "spreading kindness means spreading it to animals, too. I'd feel sorry for any dog we gave to Todd!"

"We'll just have to find some good in Todd first then," said Jessica. "I have a plan. Tonight every one of us will write down one good thing about Todd. I know it's hard, but try! And remember: there's good in everybody."

The next day, all the Goodness Gorillas stood on Todd's doorstep and rang the doorbell. Todd answered the door himself. He looked like he'd been crying. "What do you want?" he asked.

"We've come to make you a Goodness Gorilla!" said Jessica.

Todd narrowed his eyes. "Why?" he growled, looking nastier than ever.

"Let us in and we'll tell you all the reasons."

Todd turned around and stomped back into the house, but he left the door open. The Goodness Gorillas piled in, each one carrying a piece of paper.

"Todd's the fastest runner in our class," said Patricia.

"Todd has nice blue eyes," said Tina.

"Todd was friendly back in first grade," said Stuart.

"Todd is funny when he tells jokes that don't make fun of people," said Peter.

“Michael and I came up with the same reason,” said Jessica. “And it’s the best one of all: Todd does a great gorilla imitation!”

“We want to learn it!” said Michael and Tina and Peter. “We all want to be gorillas!”

“How do you make the grunts sound so real? Show us how to do the hop!” said Patricia.

Everyone tried to do Todd's gorilla dance while Todd stood and watched them. Finally he had to smile, and then laugh. They weren't making fun of him. They really wanted to learn!

When he couldn't resist any longer, Todd turned himself into a gorilla, too. Everyone followed his lead. They all grunted and hopped and scratched and screeched until they fell, out of breath and laughing, into a big heap on the floor.

Jessica said, "Now that you're one of us, Todd, we have a surprise for you!" She took Todd's arm and led him out to his backyard, where the Goodness Gorillas had tied a furry, funny, black-and-white puppy.

Todd ran over to the puppy and knelt down beside her, hugging her and stroking her fur. Big tears filled his eyes when he looked up at his new friends. "I'm sorry I made fun of you," he said. "I didn't think you would ever be this nice to me. Can I really join your club?"

The puppy jumped up and down.

"Look! She wants to be a gorilla, too!" said Tina.

"That's what I'll name her!" said Todd. "Her name can be G.G.—for Goodness Gorillas—and she can belong to the whole club, like a mascot!"

Everyone loved the idea.

The Goodness Gorillas signed up more and more members. Ms. King's class became a nicer place. Then the school became a nicer place, and then the town did.

And as the Goodness Gorillas grew up, and went to different colleges, and traveled to different cities . . . the whole world became a nicer place.

JESSiCA DOCKET for PRESIDENT
VOTE
I'm a Goodness Gorilla

The Best Night Out with Dad

Story Adapted from
"The Circus"
by Dan Clark

Story Adaptation by
Lisa McCourt

Illustrated by
Bert Dodson

"You mean you've never been to the circus before?" Danny asked the big-eyed little kid.

The boy reached for his dad's hand, looked down, and shook his head no.

Danny was sorry he'd said it like that. The boy's clothes were mended and his sneakers were almost worn through. *Maybe his family couldn't ever afford the circus before,* Danny thought.

Danny was wearing the sweatshirt his dad had bought him the last time they went to the circus. It was his favorite shirt, with a big picture of Thor, the famous circus tiger, on it. That's what the little kid had noticed. That's why he had asked Danny what the circus was like.

Thor

"What's your name?" Danny asked him.

"Vincent," said the boy, smiling again.

"Well, Vincent, get ready for the night of your life! The circus has every cool thing you can think of. First, you'll smell the popcorn and hear the big band playing. The ringmaster will come out in a shiny red coat and top hat. In his boomy voice, he'll say stuff like: 'Welcome, ladies and gentlemen, and children of all ages. . . .'

“Acrobats come tumbling out! They jump and leapfrog, and turn somersaults and cartwheels. They spin hoops on their arms and legs. The jugglers toss rings and balls and all kinds of stuff in the air and everyone parades around in their sparkly costumes.

“Then the music gets all mysterious. The lights lower almost to darkness. A blue mist creeps in and fills the ring. All of a sudden, two white horses charge out of the darkness, their flowing manes shimmering in the misty fog! They rear up on their hind legs and dance around their trainer.

"The lights go up and the music gets faster. The horses break into a speedy gallop around the ring, jumping through hoops that get higher and higher! More horses come out, with riders on them. The riders do flips off of the horses, each one landing on the horse behind her!

"The lights get low again. The music changes. The spotlight moves up, up, up, to the highwire! A woman tiptoes across.

"She stands on one leg . . . she does a split on the wire! A man walks out onto the wire, too. He does jumps and scissor-kicks. He does a backwards somers—"

"Do they ever fall off?" Vincent urgently whispered.

"Oh, sure. That's what makes the circus so dangerous and exciting."

Vincent nervously bit his lip.

Danny said, "I'm just kidding you, buddy. They almost never fall off. They're real pros."

Vincent let out a big breath.

"What else? What else?!" he begged.

“Let’s see. There’s the dogs! Yeah, the dogs do some really cool tricks.

“And the clowns! The clowns are awesome! Some walk on stilts so they look about as tall as a house. Others ride super-high unicycles or drive these wacky little cars or throw pies at each other.

"The acrobats are really cool, too! They hang from rings and twist their bodies up like pretzels. Then, on the ground, two of them clasp their arms together and toss their brother up into the air. He does somersaults in the air, then comes back and lands in their arms. They throw him up again, and he lands on his brother's shoulders. Then they each flip themselves up on top of the top guy's shoulders until they're a big human totem pole!

"And wait till you see the bears in their tutus! The dancing bears will crack you up! Some of them ride motorcycles and do wheelies. . . ."

“What about the elephants?!” asked Vincent. He was so wound up, he could barely spit the words out. “What do the elephants do?”

“Well, they dance ballet for one thing! They stand up on their hind legs and carry people around in their mouths. The coolest part is when an elephant holds a girl by his trunk and spins her around really fast.

“And the trapeze artists! They really fly! One swings across on a trapeze, then lets go. Another one catches her legs and swings her upside down. Then he lets go and she does a somersault in midair! She switches trapezes with a new guy who’s just swung in. Then, blindfolded, the new guy does a triple somersault!”

Danny's father bought their tickets and said, "Ready, sport?"

"Wait, Dad," said Danny. Then, to Vincent, he said, "But that's not even the best. The best, the very coolest act in the circus is: THOR! Wait till you see this giant cat in action!"

Vincent's eyes were as big and round as saucers. "This is gonna be the best birthday present I ever got!" he yelled.

TICKETS
Thor

Vincent hopped up and down with excitement as his dad stepped up to the window. The ticket agent shook her head. "I'm sorry, sir. The management doesn't accept this coupon anymore. You'll have to pay full price."

Vincent's father stood still.

In a small voice, Vincent said, "What's the matter, Dad? Buy the tickets!"

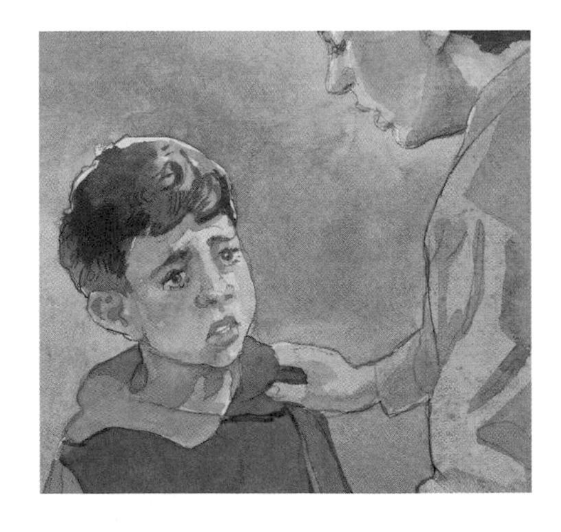

He doesn't have the money, Danny thought. His heart sank as Vincent's father closed his wallet and gently pulled Vincent out of the line. Vincent wouldn't see the circus. All of Danny's excitement melted away until he felt like crying. He looked up at his dad and whispered, "What can we do?"

Danny's father thought for a moment, then said, "You know, the courts are open late tonight, Son. Would you rather see the same old circus again or shoot some hoops, instead?" He handed Danny the two tickets he had just bought, saying, "It's up to you."

Danny understood right away. He thought about the decision his father was letting him make.

A warm, good feeling filled Danny up inside, and a smile crept across his face. "I guess I could use some practice for Saturday's game," he said.

Vincent and his father were already walking away.

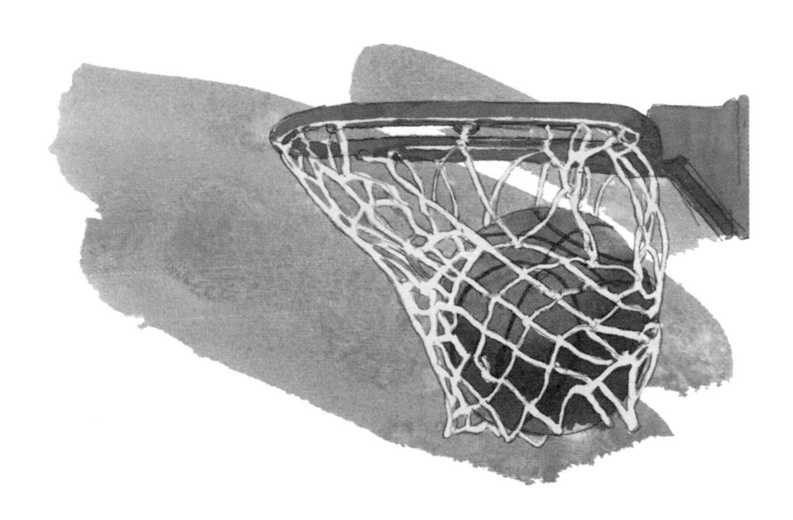

"Hey, Vincent," Danny called, running to them.

Vincent turned around, wiping his nose on his sleeve. "What?" he mumbled.

Danny saw the tear streaks on Vincent's face and for a moment he didn't know what to say.

"I really liked telling you about the circus, buddy. And I guess . . . I want you to see it more than I want to see it myself. I've got this basketball game. . . . Anyway, my dad and I are going to go practice, so it turns out we don't need these tickets after all. Really." Danny held the tickets out to Vincent.

Vincent's face lit up like Christmas. "Can we, Dad?"

Vincent's father looked at Danny with eyes full of thanks. Before the man could say anything, Danny pressed the tickets into Vincent's hand and ran back to his own dad.

BULLS

Danny's father knelt down and hugged Danny hard. He said, "You did a very kind and special thing tonight, Son. I'm so proud of you."

They didn't see the circus, but to Danny, it was the best night out with Dad ever.

The Never-Forgotten Doll

Story Adapted from
"A Doll for Great-Grandmother"
by Jacqueline Hickey

Story Adaptation by
Lisa McCourt

Illustrated by
Mary O'Keefe Young

"Ellie! What a surprise!" said Miss Maggie when she opened the door. She always said that, even though I came every day after school.

"I've just made cookies," she said. "Will you help me eat a few?"

Miss Maggie was the best sitter I'd ever had, and I'd had a lot. Mom called her my adopted grandmother, but I didn't know you could adopt a person so old.

“Tell me a story from when you were little,” I begged Miss Maggie for the gazillionth time.

“Wonderful idea! What should the story be about today?” she asked between sips of hot cocoa.

I tried to think up a new story-starter. Miss Maggie’s

stories were the best. "I know!" I said. "Tell me about your favorite toy."

Miss Maggie thought for a moment, then frowned. "I should warn you: This one isn't a happy story."

"It's okay. Tell me," I said.

"On my eighth birthday, I opened a present that I will never forget. She was the most beautiful doll I had ever seen. Her big blue eyes opened and closed on a real china face. She wore a fancy white dress with lace trim, and her long brown hair was tied back with a pink satin ribbon. Owning a doll like that was a dream come true for a poor farm girl like me. I knew my parents couldn't afford fine things. How much they must have loved me to have spent their hard-earned money on such a luxury!"

Miss Maggie got a misty look in her eyes. "Dolls back then were very fragile—their faces were made of the most delicate china. I still remember how magical it felt just to hold her. My mother lit the candles on my birthday cake and called me to the kitchen.

"I laid her down gently on the hallway table. But as I went to join my family for my birthday song, we heard the crash. I knew without looking that it was my precious doll! Her lacy dress had hung from the table just enough for my baby sister to reach up and pull on it. When I ran to the hall, there was my doll, her face smashed to pieces. My mother tried to glue her up, but it couldn't be done. She was gone forever."

I had never seen a look like that on Miss Maggie's face. I wrapped my arms around her neck and hugged her tight. The rest of the day we practiced my spelling words and played games, but I couldn't stop thinking about how unhappy Miss Maggie had looked remembering her broken doll.

Later that night, Mom said, "Saturday is Miss Maggie's birthday. Why don't you and I bake her a cake and bring it over there?"

"Oh, Mom, that's perfect!" I said. "Miss Maggie was sad today, and that's just the thing to cheer her up!"

COLLECTIBLES
BUY & SELL

The next day after school, I found an even better thing. I was walking to Miss Maggie's, just like always, when I saw a doll in the window of Mulligan's Collectibles. She looked really old and she had on a white lacy dress. Her hair was blond, not brown, and there was no pink satin ribbon, but I thought Miss Maggie might like her anyway.

I went in and asked Mr. Mulligan, "The doll in the window—do her eyes open and close?"

Mr. Mulligan said, "Yes, they do. But that's not a doll for little girls like you. That's an antique. Grown-ups collect them."

"Oh, it's not for me. I want to buy that doll for my friend, Miss Maggie," I explained.

"That's an awfully expensive present. Maybe Miss Maggie would like one of these embroidered hankies instead." Mr. Mulligan held up a dumb white handkerchief with flowers on it.

"How much for the doll?" I asked him in my most grown-up voice.

"Well, she's not in the best shape. I suppose I could let you have her for thirty-five dollars."

My eyes bugged out about a mile. Where would I ever get thirty-five dollars?

That night, I tried Mom. "May I have thirty-five dollars to buy Miss Maggie a birthday present?" I asked, real casual.

Mom laughed. "It's sweet that you want to buy a gift for your friend. But I'm sure the birthday cake we're making will be enough."

I begged and pleaded, but the best I could get out of Mom was: "If you really want to give Miss Maggie a gift that badly, we'll go shopping on Saturday morning. But we can't afford to spend thirty-five dollars. I'm sorry, darling, but we just can't."

I knew no other gift would do, so I emptied my elephant bank and counted my money. I had exactly eight dollars and forty-nine cents.

It was already Thursday. There was no time to save up any more. I put the eight dollars and forty-nine cents in a sock and folded it up. I had a plan, but I wasn't sure it would work.

On Friday after school, I went to see Mr. Mulligan.

"I really need that doll, Mr. Mulligan," I said. "I have eight dollars and forty-nine cents to pay you right now, and I will help out in your store every weekend until I have paid the rest of the money, which will probably be forever."

Mr. Mulligan scratched his head. "After you asked about that doll yesterday, I went to take another look at her. And it's the darndest thing—she's more damaged than I thought. One of my workers must have laid her head on some wet wood stain. The back of her hair is just ruined. I don't know who's going to pay much for her now. I reckon if you need her that badly, I can consider eight dollars and forty-nine cents a fair price."

"You've got a deal!" I shouted.

When Mr. Mulligan took down the doll, and showed me her "ruined" hair, I got the best idea ever!

The time passed slowly at Miss Maggie's that afternoon. When she asked me what was in the bag, I told her it was a secret and she mustn't look inside.

"Aren't you mysterious today?" she teased.

When I got home, I raced to my room and unwrapped the doll. I took out my brown magic marker. I laid the doll down and spread out her hair on a piece of construction paper.

Then, very, very carefully, I colored all of her blond hair brown. The stained part disappeared and she was even more like the doll Miss Maggie remembered!

There was only one thing missing. I took my favorite and only party dress out of my closet and laid it on my bed. There, right at the neck, was a pink satin ribbon.

I cut it off with my safety scissors, being careful to cut just the threads that held it on, and not the dress. I tied it in the doll's new brown hair. She was perfect! But what would Mom say when she found out about my dress?

On Saturday, we went to see Miss Maggie.

"Ellie, what a surprise!" she said. For once, I think she meant it.

Mom and I marched in, singing, "Happy birthday to you . . ." I could hardly wait till the song was over to give Miss Maggie her present!

Miss Maggie carefully pulled back the tissue paper. When she finally saw the doll, her eyes filled up with tears.

"Ellie," she whispered, "where on Earth . . . "

"Is she like the doll that got broken?" I asked.

"She is exactly like my doll," Miss Maggie said, without once taking her eyes off the present. "But where did you ever find her and how did you ever afford her?"

Mom was looking at me like she wanted to know the same thing, so I told them both the whole story. When I got to the part about my dress, I asked Mom, "Are you mad?"

Mom squeezed my hand and her voice cracked when she told me, "No, sugar, I'm not mad."

A tear ran down Miss Maggie's face and she said, "Now I know how it is possible that this doll looks just like the one I held in my arms exactly eighty years ago today. Both dolls were gotten from pure love. And love, wherever it comes from, always looks the same."

The cake was delicious, and Miss Maggie said it was her favorite birthday yet.